THE GREEDY MOTHER-IN-LAW

HEY SAUMITRI! CLEAN THEM WELL EH!

YES MOTHER.

.KUMATI, THE WIFE OF THE HEAD-MAN OF SALAGRAM VILLAGE, WAS A TYRANT. SHE DERIVED SPECIAL PLEASURE IN TORMENTING HER SIMPLE DAUGHTER-IN-LAW SAUMITRI.

SAUMITRI SLOGGED FROM MORNING TILL NIGHT AND YET COULD NEVER PLEASE HER MOTHER-IN-LAW.

COME ON SLOW POKE! WORK FASTER...

I AM GOING TO THE TEMPLE. KEEP THE FOOD READY. I WILL EAT IMMEDIATELY ON MY RETURN.

ALL RIGHT, MOTHER.

AND DON'T WASTE ANY FOOD.

YES MOTHER.

SAUMITRI IMMEDIATELY BEGAN TO COOK.

I NEVER REMAIN IDLE. STILL SHE FINDS FAULT WITH EVERYTHING I DO.

WHEN THE FOOD WAS READY—

SHE IS BACK SO SOON. I MUST OPEN THE DOOR IMMEDIATELY OTHERWISE...

KNOCK KNOCK

SHE OPENED THE DOOR AND SAW NOT HER MOTHER-IN-LAW BUT A SADHU.

MAY GOD BLESS YOU MY CHILD. WILL YOU FEED A HUNGRY SADHU?

I WOULD LIKE TO BUT...

DON'T WASTE ANY FOOD.

FEEDING A SADHU IS DHARMA, NOT WASTAGE. LET ME WELCOME HIM. I SHALL FEED HIM MY SHARE.

COME! PLEASE COME IN SIR.

THE FOOD IS DELICIOUS!

THEN PLEASE HAVE SOME MORE SIR!

THE SADHU WAS ABOUT TO FINISH HIS MEAL WHEN KUMATI RETURNED.

WHAT IS GOING ON HERE?

WE ARE NOT RUNNING A FREE KITCHEN HERE.

MOTHER!

GET OUT, YOU BEGGAR.

MOTHER! DON'T.

AND DIDN'T I TELL YOU NOT TO WASTE FOOD?

I DID NOT! I FED HIM MY SHARE.

YOU DID NOT BRING YOUR SHARE FROM YOUR FATHER'S HOUSE.

NO SADHU GOES AWAY HUNGRY FROM MY FATHER'S DOOR.

THEN GO TO YOUR FATHER'S HOUSE AND RUN A FREE KITCHEN.

MOTHER!

BANG!

3

HAVING BEEN THROWN OUT, SAUMITRI HAD NO CHOICE.

...I MUST GO TO MY FATHER.

THE PATH TO HER FATHER'S VILLAGE PASSED THROUGH A DENSE FOREST.

SUDDENLY —

CRACK

THE RAIN WAS SO HEAVY THAT THE SHELTER PROVIDED BY THE TREE BECAME INEFFECTIVE.

I WILL TAKE SHELTER IN THAT HOLLOW.

THE TREE WAS THE HOME OF TWO RAKSHASIS*.

THIS BLASTED RAIN!

I AM SICK OF GETTING WET.

THIS RAIN IS NOT GOING TO STOP. LET US GO TO SUVARNA DWEEP.

I AM TOO TIRED TO FLY.

YOU JUST RELAX. I WILL MAKE THE TREE FLY US THERE.

* DEMONESSES

SUDDENLY THE TREE STARTED FLYING. SAUMITRI WAS JOLTED OUT OF SLUMBER.

OH GOD! RAKSHASIS! WHAT SHALL I DO NOW?

THIS IS FUN.

WHEEE

SOON—

HERE WE ARE IN SUVARNA DWEEP.

THE JOURNEY HAS MADE ME HUNGRY.

LET US CATCH SOME PREY.

SAUMITRI HEAVED A SIGH OF RELIEF.

THANK GOD! THEY ARE GONE...

...AH... I WILL STEP OUT AND STRETCH MY LIMBS.

WHEN SAUMITRI STEPPED OUT ON THE BEACH—

THIS SAND GLITTERS...

IT LOOKS LIKE...

OH, IT IS... IT IS SAND OF GOLD!

I HAVE GOT ENOUGH GOLD TO LAST US FOR TWO GENERATIONS.

SOON THE DEMONESSES RETURNED.

THAT WAS A GOOD FEAST.

YES, NOW LET US GO BACK TO SALAGRAM.

AT DAY-BREAK THE TREE LANDED IN THE JUNGLE NEAR SALAGRAM.

I AM HUNGRY AGAIN.

LET US GO TO HUNT.

WHEN THE COAST WAS CLEAR, SAUMITRI STARTED FOR HER HOME.

MOTHER-IN-LAW WILL BE HAPPY TO RECEIVE ALL THIS GOLD.

THE MOMENT SAUMITRI REACHED HOME —

MOTHER! LOOK WHAT I HAVE BROUGHT!

AFTER SAUMITRI NARRATED HER STORY —

YOU BROUGHT SO LITTLE GOLD.

IT IS ENOUGH TO LAST US A LIFETIME.

GOLD IS NEVER ENOUGH.

I COULDN'T CARRY ANY MORE.

I WILL. I SHALL GO TO THE SUVARNA DWEEP WITH THE RAKSHASIS.

PLEASE DON'T, MOTHER...

...THE RAKSHASIS ARE VERY DANGEROUS. THEY EAT HUMAN FLESH.

IF A STUPID GIRL LIKE YOU COULD ESCAPE, THEY WILL NEVER FIND ME.

SOON KUMATI WAS HIDING IN THE SAME TAMARIND TREE.

NOW TO WAIT FOR THE TREE TO FLY.

AT NIGHT THE RAKSHASIS RETURNED TO THEIR TREE AND FLEW ON IT.

I WANT TO EAT SEA-FISH TONIGHT.

THEN LET US GO TO KADAL DWEEP.

THINK BEFORE YOU ACT

A CRANE AND A CRAB WERE GOOD FRIENDS.

ONE DAY —

FRIEND, THAT SNEAKING THIEF, THE SNAKE HAS EATEN UP OUR EGGS AGAIN.

OH, NO!

WE ARE HELPLESS.

YOU ARE NOT. NOT WHEN YOU HAVE A FRIEND LIKE ME.

YOU MUST GET THE SNAKE KILLED. I HAVE A PLAN.

THE CRANE LISTENED CAREFULLY AS THE CRAB UNFOLDED HIS PLAN.

I LIKE YOUR IDEA. IT MUST WORK.

I AM SURE IT WILL.

HOWEVER, THE CRANE'S WIFE WAS NOT VERY ENTHUSIASTIC.

ARE YOU SURE OF THE RESULTS? IS THERE ANY DRAWBACK IN THE PLAN? PLEASE THINK.

WE HAVE NO TIME TO THINK. WE HAVE TO ACT NOW.

THE CRANE FLEW TO THE SEASHORE.

COLLECTED A DEAD FISH LEFT BEHIND BY THE FISHERMEN...

...AND DROPPED IT NEAR THE PLACE WHERE A MONGOOSE LIVED.

HE COLLECTED ANOTHER DEAD FISH AND DROPPED IT A LITTLE DISTANCE AWAY.

I HOPE THE CRAB'S PLAN WILL WORK.

AFTER SOME TIME WHEN THE MONGOOSE CAME OUT—

I SMELL FISH.

AH, HERE IT IS.

AH, ONE MORE FISH.

WHAT, ANOTHER! TODAY IS MY LUCKY DAY.

THE MONGOOSE FOLLOWED THE TRACK OF DEAD FISH...

AND REACHED THE TREE WHERE THE CRANE LIVED.

AH, HERE HE COMES.

THE SNAKE ALSO SPOTTED HIS ENEMY.

HOW DARE HE ENTER MY TERRITORY!

A SNAKE!

IN THE FIGHT THAT FOLLOWED...

...THE SNAKE WAS KILLED...

...MUCH TO THE RELIEF OF THE CRANES.

THANK GOD! OUR EGGS ARE SAFE.

BUT THEIR HOPE WAS SHORT-LIVED. THE FOLLOWING DAY THE MONGOOSE FOLLOWED THE SAME TRACK.

WHAT! NO FISH TODAY.

LET ME CLIMB THIS TREE AND TRY MY LUCK.

WHEN THE CRANES FLEW BACK TO THEIR NEST THEY SAW THE MONGOOSE GOING DOWN THE TREE.

AND THEY FOUND THE EGGS MISSING AGAIN.

WE GOT RID OF ONE ENEMY ONLY TO INVITE ANOTHER.

THAT'S WHY WE MUST THINK CAREFULLY BEFORE WE ACT.

THE FOOLISH FROG KING

ONCE AN OLD, WEAK SNAKE CAME TO A POND FULL OF FROGS.

SO MANY FAT FROGS...

...BUT I CAN'T CATCH THEM.

ALAS! OLD AGE HAS MADE ME SLOW AND WEAK...

...AND I GROW WEAKER DAY BY DAY FOR LACK OF FOOD.

I MUST DO SOMETHING TO GET FOOD.

THE SNAKE LAY QUIETLY, PRETENDING TO BE DEAD. THE FROG PRINCE AND HIS FRIENDS WERE PASSING BY.

HEY! THE SNAKE IS NOT MOVING.

COULD IT BE DEAD?

LET US INVESTIGATE.

THE MOTHER FROG TRIED TO DISSUADE THEM.

NO, DON'T. IT WILL EAT YOU.

BUT THE FOOLHARDY FROG PRINCE DID NOT LISTEN TO HIS MOTHER.

OH! IT DIDN'T EVEN MOVE.

LET ME TRY AGAIN.

TOCK

THE SNAKE OPENED ITS EYES A SLIT.

WHATEVER YOU DO, I AM NOT GOING TO BE ANGRY...

...FROGS USED TO BE MY FAVOURITE FOOD. BUT ONCE I BIT THE SON OF A SAGE.

THE INFURIATED SAGE CURSED ME...

...TO CARRY FROGS ON MY BACK FOR THE REST OF MY LIFE.

THEN I SHALL RIDE YOU.

PLEASE DO, O PRINCE!

THE FROG PRINCE CLIMBED UP THE BACK OF THE SNAKE.

CARRY ME TO MY PARENTS.

AS YOU WISH PRINCE.

IN NO TIME THE SNAKE REACHED THE KING AND QUEEN OF FROGS.

LOOK FATHER! I AM RIDING A SNAKE.

OH! MY BRAVE SON.

LET US ALSO RIDE ON THE SNAKE.

ALL RIGHT.

UGH!

I CAN EAT THEM RIGHT NOW, BUT PATIENCE BRINGS GREATER REWARDS.

WHEE!!

HOORAY!

A FEW DAYS LATER—

HOW EXCITING!

YES. BUT HE MOVES TOO SLOW.

CAN YOU MOVE FASTER, FRIEND?

I CAN'T, O KING! I HAVE NOT EATEN FOR SEVERAL DAYS.

WHY DIDN'T YOU? THE ROYAL VEHICLE MUST BE WELL FED.

BUT I CAN'T EAT WITHOUT YOUR PERMISSION.

CAN'T EAT WITHOUT MY PERMISSION...

18

20

NO! NO! I WANT MY SNAKE. I WANT MY SNAKE.

NOW, NOW, SON! DON'T BE ANGRY. YOUR FATHER WILL TAKE CARE OF THINGS.

DON'T BE SO CRUEL. YOU ARE BREAKING THE PRINCE'S HEART.

BUT...

NO BUTS! LET THE SNAKE EAT SOME FROGS!!

ALL RIGHT! ALL RIGHT!

SO, WITH THE KING'S PERMISSION THE SNAKE STARTED EATING THE FROGS.

AND THE SNAKE BECAME STRONGER.

WEE E

SOON—

I AM HUNGRY, O KING.

THEN EAT SOME FROGS.

BUT NONE ARE LEFT.

SO. I AM NOW A KING WITHOUT SUBJECTS.

BUT STILL YOU HAVE A UNIQUE ROYAL MOUNT.

AND THE ROYAL MOUNT IS HUNGRY...

... AND SINCE NO MORE FROGS ARE LEFT I WILL EAT YOU.

AND THE SNAKE KILLED THE KING, QUEEN AND PRINCE FROGS.

THE PRETENTIOUS OWL

KANAKAKSHA*, THE OWL, HAD AN EXTRAORDINARY FRIEND IN SUMITRA, THE KING OF SWANS.

GREETINGS, FRIEND SUMITRA...

GREETINGS, KANAKAKSHA.

I SHALL BE WITH YOU IN A MOMENT. LET ME SETTLE A DISPUTE AMONG MY SUBJECTS.

I'LL WAIT HERE.

KANAKAKSHA HAD TOLD SUMITRA THAT HE TOO WAS A KING.

HE WILL SHUN ME IF HE KNEW THAT I AM A POOR OWL.

I MUST DO SOMETHING TO PROVE THAT I TOO AM A KING.

* GOLDEN EYED.

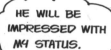

NO! TODAY! IF YOU VALUE MY FRIENDSHIP.

SO KANAKAKSHA PREVAILED UPON SUMITRA TO VISIT HIS ABODE.

THIS IS MY DOMAIN AND THESE ARE MY MEN.

AH! MAGNIFICENT.

HE IS LYING. BUT I WILL NOT HURT HIS FEELINGS.

MY MEN ARE TOTALLY LOYAL TO ME.

GOOD. ARE THEY PROCEEDING ON A MARCH?

NO.

BUT THEY ARE LEAVING.

HOW CAN THEY WITHOUT MY ORDERS!

AND THE OWL HOOTED.

HO OO HO OO.

OWL HOOTING! IT IS A BAD OMEN. LET US POSTPONE OUR DEPARTURE.

AND THE ARMY UNPACKED.

THERE! YOU SEE MY MEN ARE VERY OBEDIENT.

YES! YES!

SINCE HE IS MY FRIEND I WILL HUMOUR HIM.

NEXT MORNING—

OOOO

STUPID MEN. THEY DID NOT OBEY MY ORDER.

AND THE OWL HOOTED AGAIN.

HOO. HOO.

DRAT THAT OWL. WE HAVE TO POSTPONE OUR MARCH AGAIN.

I WILL PULL UP MY GENERAL FOR INDISCIPLINE.

HE IS GOING TOO FAR.

BUT, WHEN THE OWL HOOTED AGAIN ON THE THIRD DAY TO PREVENT THE ARMY'S DEPARTURE—

HOO. HOO.

BLAST THAT OWL. WILL SOME ONE TAKE CARE OF THIS ILL-OMEN MAKER?

Boats, Ships and Ports of Ancient India

Script : Swarn Khandpur ● Illustrations : Ramesh Umrotkar

SHIPPING IN INDIA IS AS OLD AS HER HISTORY. THE REMAINS OF A LARGE DOCKYARD AT LOTHAL (GUJARAT) SHOW THAT THE SHIPPING INDUSTRY FLOURISHED DURING THE INDUS VALLEY CIVILIZATION.
A SEAL OF MOHENJODARO TIMES FOUND IN MESOPOTAMIA HAS A SHIP MOTIF.

IN ANCIENT TIMES, SHIPS WERE NAVIGATED WITH THE HELP OF OARS AND RUDDERS. SOME HAD MASTS. PROWS WERE OF VARIOUS SHAPES AND STUDDED WITH PRECIOUS STONES.

THIS CARVING FROM BHARHUT (NEAR SANCHI) SHOWS TWO BOATS WITH THREE SAILORS IN EACH. ONE OF THE BOATS IS BEING SWALLOWED BY A SEA-MONSTER.

AND THIS PAINTING AT AJANTA DEPICTS THE SHIP IN WHICH KING VIJAYA AND HIS 700 FOLLOWERS SET OUT FOR SINHALA (SRI LANKA) FROM BENGAL.

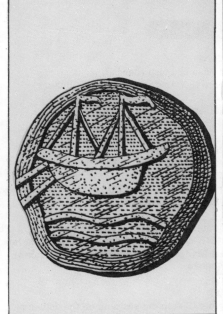

THE EARLY ANDHRAS OF THE 2ND AND 3RD CENTURIES A.D. ISSUED COINS BEARING IMAGES OF SHIPS.

THE PEOPLE OF THE EAST COAST ALSO COLONIZED JAVA AND SUMATRA. THIS CARVING OF A SHIP AT THE BOROBUDUR TEMPLE CLOSELY RESEMBLES THE CATAMARAN USED TODAY ALONG THE COROMANDEL COAST. THE WORD 'CATAMARAN' LITERALLY MEANS 'BOUND LOGS' IN TAMIL.

SUBSCRIBE NOW!

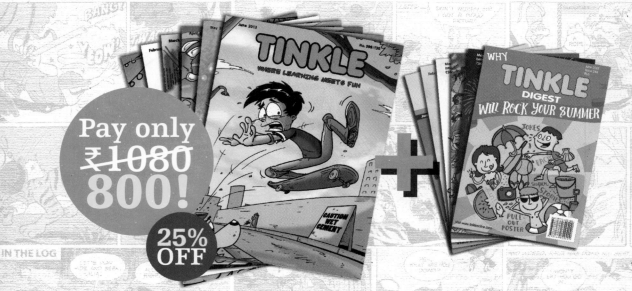

Pay only ₹~~1080~~ 800!
25% OFF

A twelve month subscription to
TINKLE and TINKLE DIGEST

YOUR DETAILS*

Student's Name _____

Parent's Name _____

Date of Birth: _____ (DD MM YYYY)

Address: _____

_____

_____

City: _____ PIN: _____

State: _____

School: _____

Class: _____

Email (Student): _____

Email (Parent): _____

Tel of Parent: (R): _____

Mobile: _____

_____
Parent's Signature:

*All the above fields are mandatory for the subscription to get activated.

PAYMENT OPTIONS

☐ **Credit Card**
Card Type: Visa ☐ MasterCard ☐
Please charge ₹800 to my Credit Card Number
below: ☐☐☐☐ ☐☐☐☐ ☐☐☐☐ ☐☐☐☐
Expiry Date: ☐☐ ☐☐

_____
Cardmember's Signature:

☐ **CHEQUE / DD**
Enclosed please find cheque / DD no. ☐☐☐☐☐☐ drawn
favour of "ACK Media Direct Pvt. Ltd."
on (bank) _____
for the amount _____, dated ☐☐/☐☐/☐☐☐☐ a
send it to: **IBH magazine Service, Arch no.30, Below
Mahalaxmi Bridge, Near Racecourse, Mahalaxmi,
Mumbai 400034**

☐ **Pay by VPP**
Please pay the ₹800 to the postman on the delivery
of 1st issue. (Additional charges ₹30 apply)

☐ **Online subscription**
Visit www.amarchitrakatha.com

For any queries or further information please
write to us ACK Media Direct Pvt. Ltd.,
Krishna House, 3rd Floor, Raghuvanshi Mills Compund,
Senapati Bapat Marg, Lower Parel, Mumbai 400 013.
Tel: 022-40 49 74 36
or send us an Email at customercare@ack-media.com